MW01244993

SandCastle

Do Something About It!

Do Something in Your World

Amanda Rondeau

Consulting Editor, Diane Craig, M.A./Reading Specialist

ABDO
Publishing Company

Published by ABDO Publishing Company, 4940 Viking Drive, Edina, Minnesota 55435.

Printed in the United States.

Credits
Edited by: Pam Price
Curriculum Coordinator: Nancy Tuminelly
Cover and Interior Design and Production: Mighty Media
Photo Credits: Comstock, Corbis Images, Digital Vision, Photo Alto, PhotoDisc, Stockbyte, Skjold Photography

Library of Congress Cataloging-in-Publication Data

Rondeau, Amanda, 1974-.
   Do something in your world / Amanda Rondeau.
   p. cm.--(Do something about it!)
   Includes index.
   ISBN 1-59197-576-X
   1. Child volunteers--Juvenile literature. 2. Social action--Juvenile literature. 3. Community development--Juvenile literature. 4. Quality of life--Juvenile literature. I. Title. II. Series.

   HQ784.V64 R663 2004
   361--dc21
                                                                          2003058390

SandCastle™ books are created by a professional team of educators, reading specialists, and content developers around five essential components that include phonemic awareness, phonics, vocabulary, text comprehension, and fluency. All books are written, reviewed, and leveled for guided reading, early intervention reading, and Accelerated Reader® programs and designed for use in shared, guided, and independent reading and writing activities to support a balanced approach to literacy instruction.

Let Us Know

After reading the book, SandCastle would like you to tell us your stories about reading. What is your favorite page? Was there something hard that you needed help with? Share the ups and downs of learning to read. We want to hear from you! To get posted on the ABDO Publishing Company Web site, send us e-mail at:

sandcastle@abdopub.com

SandCastle Level: Transitional

You can make a difference in the world by doing something to make it a better place to live.

When you do something to help others, you are making a difference.

Ms. Wilson wants all kids to get a good education.

She teaches English at a school in Brazil.

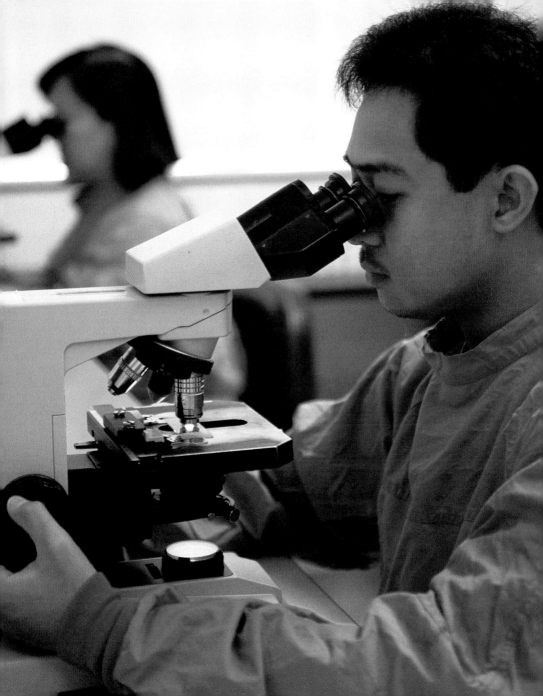

Mr. Tran wants to help people who have cancer.

He is working to find a cure.

Mr. and Mrs. Long want to learn about different countries.

They learn about Spain while on vacation there.

Mr. Young wants his daughter to meet people from around the world.

He invites a student from Israel to stay with them.

Lisa wants to learn about life in another country.

She is pen pals with a girl in Kenya.

Steve worries about the air around the world getting polluted.

He plants a tree because trees make oxygen to help keep the air clean.

Doug and Brian worry about people in other countries who are hungry.

They sell lemonade to raise money to buy food.

Many people in the world do not have medicine when they need it.

Jackie and her friends wash cars to raise money for medicine.

There are many ways you can make a difference in the world.

What would you like to do?

Glossary

cancer. a disease that causes some cells in the body to grow faster than normal and attack healthy organs and tissues

country. a nation with its own government

education. the knowlege and skills gained in school or through other training

invite. to ask someone to do something or go somewhere with you

lemonade. a drink made from water, lemon juice, and sugar

medicine. a drug used to cure or prevent disease

oxygen. a colorless gas found in air, water, and most rocks and minerals

pen pal. a friend, usually in another state or country, with whom you exchange letters

student. someone who studies in school or on his or her own

vacation. time off from school or work, often spent traveling, relaxing, and having fun

world. the planet Earth

About SandCastle™

A professional team of educators, reading specialists, and content developers created the SandCastle™ series to support young readers as they develop reading skills and strategies and increase their general knowledge. The SandCastle™ series has four levels that correspond to early literacy development in young children. The levels are provided to help teachers and parents select the appropriate books for young readers.

Emerging Readers
(no flags)

Beginning Readers
(1 flag)

Transitional Readers
(2 flags)

Fluent Readers
(3 flags)

These levels are meant only as a guide. All levels are subject to change.

To see a complete list of SandCastle™ books and other nonfiction titles from ABDO Publishing Company, visit **www.abdopub.com** or contact us at:

4940 Viking Drive, Edina, Minnesota 55435 • 1-800-800-1312 • fax: 1-952-831-1632